Compassion

How Dalia Put a Big Yellow Comforter Inside a Tiny Blue Box

How Dalia Put a Big Yellow Comforter Inside a Tiny Blue Box

And Other Wonders of Tzedakah

Illustrations by
STACEY DRESSEN MCQUEEN

by LINDA HELLER

TRICYCLE PRESS
BERKELEY

Dalia liked to learn things and make things, and she did just that at the community center.

One Monday, her teacher, Mrs. Kahn, showed her and the other children a photograph of a little silver house that stood on four tiny feet.

She showed them a photograph of a miniature silver castle. She put a little wooden barrel and a small tin box on the table.

"These are tzedakah boxes," she said. "And if you make your own tzedakah box and fill it, you'll be amazed by what we can do."

When Dalia got home she ran to her room. She found a little box. She made a slot in its lid. She painted the box. Afterwards, and most importantly, she wrote the Hebrew letters *Tsadee Daled Kof Hay* on its front.

She took a dollar from her birthday money, dropped it through the slot, and placed the box on her shelf.

Her little brother, Yossi, saw the box. "What's in it?" he asked.

"A big yellow comforter," Dalia answered, with a look that said big sisters know so much more than their little brothers do.

"But how can a big yellow comforter fit into such a tiny box?" Yossi was just learning his Hebrew letters. "Is *Tsadee Daled Kof Hay* a magic word?"

"*Tsadee Daled Kof Hay* spells *tzedakah*. And it means I'm happy when you're happy," Dalia said. Not only was she Yossi's big sister but she was also his very smart teacher.

On Tuesday, Dalia earned fifty cents for weeding the garden. She took a quarter from her earnings and dropped it through the slot. "Now there's a big yellow comforter and a butterfly bush inside the box," she told Yossi.

"But how can a big yellow comforter and a butterfly bush fit inside a little box?" Yossi asked. He'd whispered *Tsadee Daled Kof Hay* to his own yellow blanket and the letters had not made it shrink. "Tell me the truth," he said. "What does *tzedakah* mean?"

"*Tzedakah* means I'm planting a kiss on your cheek," Dalia said.

On Wednesday, Dalia sold lemonade.
She slid five nickels through the slot
and listened to them fall.

"Now there's a big yellow comforter, a butterfly bush, and a banana cream pie inside the box," she told Yossi. "And I know just what you're going to ask. *Tzedakah* means we're all one big family. It means I want your wishes to come true. It means I care for you."

Yossi peered into the box. He shook it and heard the coins rattle. "It's just a bank," he said. He had his own bank and he knew not to make up lies about it.

"It's not a bank," Dalia said. "It's a tzedakah box. *Tzedakah* means fairness. It means doing the right thing. It means thinking of others and giving them what they need. Because of that, there are kisses and wishes and hugs in this box, along with a big yellow comforter, a butterfly bush, and a banana cream pie."

Yossi's lip quivered. He wanted to believe her. He loved his big sister.

"Actually," Dalia said, "my kisses and wishes and hugs are in the box along with part of the money for a big yellow comforter, a butterfly bush, and a banana cream pie. We're going to buy those things once our boxes are full. I want you to come with us."

On Thursday, Dalia and Yossi took turns carrying the little box to the community center.

Other children had brought their tzedakah boxes too.

"This is my brother Yossi," Dalia announced. "I'm teaching him all about tzedakah."

צדקה

Yossi helped the children count the money. At the linen store, he was the first to spot a soft yellow comforter.

At the nursery, he learned that butterfly bushes got their name because butterflies love to drink their nectar.

At the bakery, Mrs. Kahn allowed him, a boy who was three years younger than the other children, to place the order.

"One banana cream pie, please," he said.

Back at the community center, Mrs. Kahn passed out special markers and the children drew on the fabric. She found sprinkles and the children made hearts on the pie.

Yossi was having a wonderful time.

"Tomorrow will be even better," Dalia told him.

"How will it be better?" he asked.

"Wait and see," Dalia answered.

Gertie

The next day, Mrs. Kahn led the parade of children to a house where the yard looked sad and the old woman who sat on the porch looked even sadder.

"Pay attention," Dalia whispered to Yossi. "This is the important part."

"Hello, Mrs. Ross," Mrs. Kahn called. "We've come to visit."

"What a nice surprise," Mrs. Ross said. "I've been sitting here wishing I had visitors."

The children tucked the big yellow comforter around Mrs. Ross's thin legs.

"At my age I'm usually cold," Mrs. Ross said. "But wrapped in this beautiful comforter, I feel the warmth of your hearts."

The children planted the butterfly bush where Mrs. Ross could see it. Within minutes, a flock of white butterflies flew to its blossoms.

"I've never seen anything as lovely," Mrs. Ross said. "Aside from your smiling faces."

"We're not done!" Dalia shouted.

She cut the banana cream pie. Yossi served Mrs. Ross a great big piece.

"When I woke up this morning I never guessed that today would be so grand," Mrs. Ross said. "People care about me and I won't forget that again. Thank you so very much."

"Tsadee Daled Kof Hay," Yossi sang. *"Tsadee Daled Kof Hay. Tsadee Daled Kof Hay."* He turned to his sister.

"I know just what you're going to ask," Dalia said. She was his big sister, his smart teacher, and she loved him very much. "And yes, as soon as we get home I'll show you how to make your own tzedakah box."

Tzedakah Boxes

The word *tzedakah* comes from the Hebrew word *tzedek*, meaning "justice" or "fairness." Many people need help and the Judaic tradition of tzedakah reminds us that it is right and just to help them. It is everyone's happy duty to help others no matter how little we have ourselves.

Two thousand years ago, the First Temple in Jerusalem needed to be repaired. The High Priest made a hole in a box, people put money in it, and the tradition of tzedakah boxes was born. As time passed, many synagogues carried on the tradition and had large tzedakah boxes of their own. Some of the money was used to keep the synagogue in good condition while the rest helped people in the community. In the 1700s, families began to keep little tzedakah boxes in their kitchens and put money in them before every meal. When Jews came to America they brought the tradition of tzedakah boxes with them. Those who spoke Yiddish called a tzedakah box a *pushkah* which means "box" or "can."

Today, many children make tzedakah boxes at Hanukkah and on their birthdays to share the coins and bills they've received with those in need. They give tzedakah on their bat or bar mitzvah. They raise money to help poor children and sick children throughout the year because they realize that every day becomes a special day when they give tzedakah. No child is ever too young to help others. Even a few pennies can be a wonderful sign of love.

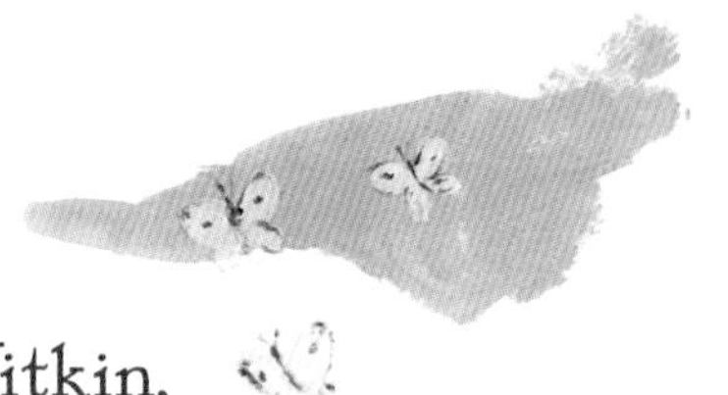

For my grandmother Sarah Witkin,
who sold her jewelry to help the poor.
—L.H.

With lots of love, hugs, and kisses
to Rob, Finn, and Emma.
—S.D.M.

 Published in the United States by Tricycle Press,
an imprint of Random House Children's Books, a division of Random House, Inc., New York.
www.randomhouse.com/kids

Library of Congress Cataloging-in-Publication Data

Heller, Linda.
How Dalia put a big yellow comforter inside a tiny blue box: and other wonders of tzedakah / by Linda Heller ;
illustrations by Stacey Dressen McQueen. — 1st ed.
p. cm.
Summary: After learning about the Jewish tradition of tzedakah boxes,
Dalia shares her knowledge with her younger brother, Yossi, by telling him what her savings can help
to provide for someone in need. Includes a note about the history and customs of tzedakah boxes.
[1. Charity—Fiction. 2. Judaism—Customs and practices—Fiction. 3. Brothers and sisters—Fiction.
4. Jews—Fiction.] I. Dressen-McQueen, Stacey, ill. II. Title.
PZ7.H37424Hp 2011
[E]—dc22
2010024325

ISBN 978-1-58246-378-0 (hardcover)
ISBN 978-1-58246-402-2 (Gibraltar lib. bdg.)
ISBN 978-1-58246-382-7 (PJ Library)

Printed in Malaysia

Design by Katie Jennings
Typeset in Hombre & Colwell
The illustrations in this book were rendered in acrylic and oil pastel.

1 2 3 4 5 6 — 16 15 14 13 12 11

First Edition

Joy

Fairness